Tree Tall and the Whiteskins

Little Pine

Grandmother

Gray Seal

Tree Tall

Bright Sky

Soldiers

Beaver Hunters

Jerome's Family

Tree Tall and the Whiteskins

Shirlee Evans
Illustrated by James Ponter

HERALD PRESS
Scottdale, Pennsylvania
Waterloo, Ontario

Library of Congress Cataloging-in-Publication Data

Evans, Shirlee, 1931-
Tree Tall and the whiteskins.

Summary: Tree Tall, an Indian boy whose family is
forced onto a reservation in nineteenth-century
Oregon, learns that not all whiteskins are alike when
his white friend Jerome teaches him about Jesus.
[1. Indians of North America—Oregon—Fiction.
2. Christian life—Fiction. 3. Oregon—Fiction]
I. Ponter, James J., ill. II. Title.
PZ7.E8925Tr   1985   [FIC]   85-13952
ISBN 0-8361-3402-8 (pbk.)

The paper used in this publication is recycled and meets the
minimum requirements of American National Standard for
Information Sciences—Permanance of Paper for Printed
Library Materials, ANSI Z39.48-1984.

TREE TALL AND THE WHITESKINS
Copyright © 1985 by Herald Press, Scottdale, Pa. 15683
  Released simultaneously in Canada by Herald Press,
  Waterloo, Ont. N2L 6H7. All rights reserved.
Library of Congress Catalog Card Number: 85-13952
International Standard Book Number: 0-8361-3402-8
Printed in the United States of America
Design by Alice Shetler

99 98 97 96 95 94 93 92 91 90 10 9 8 7 6 5 4 3 2

To Jaime and Casey,
who first heard the story of Tree Tall
at Royal Ridges Day Camp—
before it was a book.

Contents

Tree Tall and the Whiteskins

1

Strange Whiteskins

TREE TALL crept through the high dew-damp grass along the creek bank. It was early. The sun was not yet over the hill. A frog had croaked by the water's edge as Tree Tall trailed his mother down the path from their village just minutes before. She was behind him now busily picking the wild blackberries that grew thick along the creek bank.

The twelve-year-old Indian boy supposed his mother would call him soon to "stop his fooling around" and come help her pick the berries.

He leaned forward on his knees, parting the grass with his hands. Tree Tall wore only a loin-piece of elk hide. His long black hair fell loose on either side of his face. If that old frog would just croak again Tree Tall knew he could catch it. He waited. He was good at waiting. His mother had told him waiting would be his friend if he learned not to want things too soon—before the time was ripe—like the berries she had been waiting to pick.

Croak!

There it was—the frog. He could see it. The boy tensed, ready to leap down the bank after it.

"Tree Tall? Where did you go?" his mother called. "Come help fill the basket with berries."

Splash!

The pool by the edge of the swift-running water ringed with ripples where the frog had vanished. The boy sighed. That was the way with mothers. They always wanted you when you were right in the middle of things.

Getting to his feet Tree Tall went to where his mother, Little Pine, was picking berries. She glanced at him. "Come now. If we hurry I can cook these and have them drying by the time the sun is high. We will need lots of berries to help get us through the times of the long rains. Later we will dig roots."

As with most Indian women of his tribe, Little Pine wore a simple short skirt and capelike garment she had made of cedar bark. During the warm months along the Northwest Pacific Coast his people shunned clothing. Only in times of the long wet days did they cover themselves with robes woven of the inner strips of cedar tree bark, or sometimes with skins.

Stooping, the boy began plucking the soft juice-swollen berries from their thorny vines. "When I am truly tall I will not have to pick berries."

"And what will you do then?" Little Pine asked, a laugh hidden in her voice.

"I will hunt the deer and the elk like my father, Gray Seal, used to do. Maybe I will even hunt the white-skinned men who hurt Gray Seal. Then they will never hurt Indian hunters again."

Little Pine stopped her work. She straightened her back, looking at her son. "So. You have heard what happened."

Tree Tall nodded. "Why did the whiteskins hurt Gray Seal?"

"How did you hear about the whiteskins?" his mother asked.

"I heard Spotted Elk talking with another man of our village. Spotted Elk said he was with Gray Seal. They were hunting for the elk when they came upon some men with washed-out colored skin. These strange men carried long sticks they called rifles. The sticks threw fire from the end. They pointed them at Spotted Elk and Gray Seal. After the long sticks spoke, Gray Seal could not walk."

Little Pine began picking berries again. "Yes," she said. "That is how it happened."

"Why did they do it?" asked Tree Tall.

His mother shook her head. "I do not know. I have never seen men like these. But I have heard more and more of them come into our valleys and forests. They cut many trees."

"We burn through trees to make them fall to build our lodges," Tree Tall reminded her.

"But these men not only build lodges, they dig out the tree roots and turn the ground upside down," she said. "They push seeds into the earth and grow plants we have never seen before. They feed their horses and elklike animals they call cows with these strange plants. They cook other plants over the fire for their own food. They are very different from us."

"Why do they do all that work when there is grass for their horses and elklike cows?" Tree Tall asked. "Don't they know there are fish—big salmon—in the waters and berries and nuts and roots and deer and elk to eat? Don't they know about the clams and other shell food by the edge of the big waters that roar beyond the clearing where the sun disappears?"

"I have heard there are many of these whiteskins. They want more than we are used to having." Little Pine shook her head in sadness. "They want all of our forests. Someday they would push us back into the salty waves out beyond the sands if they could."

She bent to her work again. "Come now. We must pick the berries so we can return to our lodge. Your grandmother will have the trout you caught last night roasting over the fire by the time we get back. If you had a sister you would not have to do the work of the girl, as well as that of the boy. But there is no sister. Gray Seal cannot hunt. So you must help."

Tree Tall knew his mother longed for a daughter. But right now he was thinking more about Gray Seal and the whiteskins. Why would anyone want to hurt his father? Gray Seal had only been hunting the elk so his mother could roast it over the fire for them to eat, drying the rest for times when there was no fresh meat. Who were these white-skinned men and where had they come from?

Ever since Gray Seal had been hurt Tree Tall had tried to help his mother and grandmother more. It was hard for the women to gather enough food for them all to eat, as well as trying to keep their cedar plank lodge in repair.

His father had been hurt by the whiteskins just before the first heavy rains rolled in from the wide salt waters the time before. Now Gray Seal seldom talked. He spent his time sitting, carving pieces of cedar into bowls and figures of animals. When he walked at all he used a long pole with a forked end to help him hobble about.

At last Little Pine's basket was filled with blackberries. Tree Tall led the way up the path toward their village. He glanced at his mother.

Both were careful not to step on hidden berry vines—their people wore nothing on their feet. His mother's basket of berries hung from a wide strap of woven inner bark around her neck and one shoulder. The basket was one of Little Pine's favorites, woven with the pattern of a seal. But then all of Little Pine's baskets were works of skill. None of the other women of their village made such beautiful nor durable baskets. Little Pine wove them so tight that not a single drop of water could ooze through when she dropped hot cooking rocks in to boil their food.

As they came into the clearing Tree Tall saw his grandmother squatting by the fire in front of their lodge. His father sat with his back against the rough cedar boards of the lodge. As usual he was chipping at a chunk of wood with a sharpened stone and a beaver-tooth chisel.

Gray Seal's head was bare. His loose un-combed hair fell in a tangled mat on either side of his face. He also wore only a leather loin-piece. He had once been a proud, powerfully built red man. Since being hurt, he had lost all interest in life—even in keeping himself clean, forsaking his people's custom of a daily early morning bath in the creek. Only once in awhile would Gray Seal join Spotted Elk in the sweathouse now, ending the time there with a plunge into the cool waters of the creek.

16

Tree Tall's grandmother looked up as they approached. The boy glanced at the four other lodges in their village. Most of the women had the morning meal already out of the way. There were no men around now. Theirs was a small village. Tree Tall liked it that way, except that there were no boys or girls his age to play with. Most of the people were related in some way.

"I have news, daughter," Tree Tall's grandmother spoke as he and Little Pine stopped by the fire. The old woman's hair was flecked with white. She stood up slowly, placing a hand on her hip, fingering her bark strip skirt. When she did that Tree Tall knew she was not pleased.

She glanced at him, then spoke to Little Pine again. "Send the boy back to see if you have dropped berries from your basket."

Tree Tall knew there were words his grandmother wanted to say—words she did not want him to hear. They always sent him to do something unimportant when they wanted to talk so he could not hear.

"What is it, Mother?" Little Pine asked. Her voice sounded tired.

"It is about the washed-out looking ones," his grandmother spoke, glancing toward Gray Seal.

Little Pine put her basket of berries down and then slowly straightened. "Tree Tall knows about them. You can talk in front of him."

"Good. The boy should know what happened

to his father. It is only right. He is old enough to know what awaits us all at their hands."

"So, what is it about the whiteskins now?" Little Pine asked.

"They are near. I just heard. Spotted Elk came running into the village while you were gone. Before he left again with the other men he told about a camp of whiteskins on the other side of the hill. They are putting up a lodge they call a tent. There is a woman and some young whiteskins. There is a rifle in their camp. Spotted Elk said some of them have hair the color of dry grass. Your man," she again glanced at Gray Seal, "has spoken not one word since Spotted Elk returned with the news."

An unknown dread filled Tree Tall's chest. They had always been at war with other Indian tribes. He was used to that. But from what he had learned, the white-skinned people were different. Something bad—he didn't know what—was about to happen. Tree Tall could feel it.

2

The Long Stick
Speaks

LITTLE PINE poked at a fish roasting on a stick set over the fire. "Is it ready to eat? I'm hungry."

The old woman stomped her bare foot. "Are you not hearing my words, daughter? The whiteskins are—"

"Yes," Little Pine interrupted. "I heard you, Mother. There is nothing I can do. I cannot frighten them away or imagine they did not hurt Tree Tall's father. I cannot make it as though it did not happen. I can only wait to see what will come."

The gray-haired woman muttered to herself as Little Pine placed some cooked trout on a carved wooden plate and carried it to Gray Seal. Tree Tall could not make out the old woman's words, but she seemed to be full of hate for the white-skinned people. He supposed he hated them too. After all, they should not have hurt his father. And yet he was curious about them. Why was their skin so different? And why could they not be satisfied with what the land and waters gave them to eat as the Indian was?

As Tree Tall sat by the fire with the two women eating the trout he had caught the evening before, his grandmother commented, "The whiteskins will kill us all."

The boy looked at her. "The Indians kill and hurt one another. Those who are not of our tribe. Our skin is all the same color, and yet we steal and hurt when there seems no need."

Neither his grandmother nor Little Pine responded. Perhaps there was nothing they could say, for they knew it was true. Tree Tall decided it was probably the bad spirits that caused the whiteskins and the Indians to do hurtful things. His people believed the good spirits of their dead ancestors returned in the form of the cedar tree and the salmon and animals to strengthen them by providing food. But there were also bad spirits who brought trouble, sickness, and death.

Soon there was nothing left of the trout but bones. Tree Tall asked if he could go back to the creek to hunt for frogs before he had to go with his mother to dig roots. Little Pine nodded. He thought she seemed troubled. He guessed she was more worried about the whiteskins than she had said.

Tree Tall entered the trees again. But instead of going back to the creek he sat down under a fir tree to think. He looked up. The tree was strong, reaching high up toward the sky. He had been named after such a tree. If he was truly as strong as the tree he would chase all the whiteskins away. Still, that would not give his father two strong legs again. He knew life was hard for his mother and grandmother since his father could not hunt.

At last Tree Tall stood to his feet. He wanted to see the whiteskins. He wanted to see what they looked like. Maybe then he would know why they had hurt his father and wished to drive his people into the sea with their long sticks that spoke with fire.

Glancing back toward his lodge he saw his mother place a hot cooking stone in a basket with the berries. Afterward she would spread the berry pulp onto a woven mat to dry for the wet days to come. Maybe she would not miss him if he ran fast and then hurried right back. His grandmother had said the whiteskins were just over the hill. He knew a path that led there. It would not take him long if he ran fast. He had followed the path before.

Tree Tall started toward the path that led over the tree covered hill behind his village. He would have to hurry. When he reached the path he followed it at an easy trot. Tree Tall had learned he could run at that pace for a long time without getting tired.

As he ran he wondered about the whiteskins. Although his people did not have horses, he had seen other Indians from across the far mountains riding them. He had longed for a horse of his own. But he had never seen the elklike cow. He had heard the men talk of them. It was said the cow had thick round horns and moved slowly, not swiftly like the deer.

Spotted Elk said cows were used for pulling the whiteskins' lodge that rolled on wheels and for turning the ground upside down to plant their seeds. The whiteskins took milk from their cows, too. It was said they drank it. Tree Tall would like to see such an animal.

By the time he reached the top of the hill he was breathing hard. He had forgotten how far it was to the other side. His mother would be looking for him soon. Just a little farther and he would be able to see the whiteskins for himself. Then he would go right back to his village.

Tree Tall started running again. He ran swiftly down the twisting path on the other side of the hill. He seemed to be flying like a hawk now. He stretched his arms out wide, pretending he was looking for a mouse from high in the sky.

He was having such a good time that he forgot where he was going—and what was ahead of him. All of a sudden the path opened into a clearing at the bottom of the tree-lined hill. Before Tree Tall could stop his flying feet, he stumbled into something.

It was a man! Tree Tall looked down at the hands that gripped him. They were a pale color—not white like the winter's snow, but not the good reddish brown of his own skin. The boy looked up. The pale-skinned man had dark hair on his head and face, but his eyes were like the summer's sky. It was a whiteskin!

"Hold it there, young fellow," the man said.

Tree Tall could not understand the words. They sounded strange to his ears. The boy turned to race back to the forest, but the man held him by the shoulders. Tree Tall twisted to get away.

"What have you there?" a woman's voice said.

Tree Tall looked toward the woman who talked words that had no meaning to his ears. She *did* have hair the color of dry grass. It was all twisted up on the back of her head. These whiteskins wore strange coverings. Maybe they were ashamed of the whiteness of their skin.

The boy turned again to the white-skinned man with the dark hair growing on his face. Indian men kept their faces free of hair by pulling it out. This man also wore a head covering with a ledge around it that shaded his eyes from the sun. He was indeed an unusual sight!

Then Tree Tall saw a boy and girl standing close to the lodge Spotted Elk had called a tent. They too had their white bodies covered. Their hair was the color of dry summer grass also. Behind the tent grazed three animals. They were large with long fat horns on either side of their heads.

"What are you going to do with him?" the white boy asked.

"I don't rightly know," answered the man. "He doesn't appear hungry, but I'd say one of your mother's hot biscuits might prove something about us. I'd like to know where he comes from."

Tree Tall looked from one to the other as the whiteskins talked, wondering what their words meant. Then the man led him toward the tent, picking up a round object from a heavy black thing beside the fire shaped like one of his mother's cooking baskets. The man spread a creamy sun-colored something on it and handed it to Tree Tall. Then the man picked up another round object and took a large bite, chewing it as though it tasted good.

"Eat," the whiteskin said, showing Tree Tall what he meant.

The Indian boy tasted the round bread uneasily. It was good to his tongue. The woman placed a spoonful of berry mixture on his biscuit. It tasted sweeter than any berries he had ever eaten.

He looked at the four whiteskins as he ate. The man had let go of him, but had backed him against the side of the tent. If he tried to run he knew the man would stop him.

"How far do you live from here?" the man asked, making signs so Tree Tall could understand.

The boy was used to talking in sign language. His grandmother had taught him. That was in case he was ever captured by a warlike tribe who did not speak with the words of his people.

Tree Tall pointed in the direction from where he had come. He noticed how far the sun had slipped in the sky since he had left his village. He told this to the whiteskin by stretching his arms wide and pointing to show how far the sun had moved.

The man nodded. "He lives nearby. We do not want trouble with his people."

He spoke to the woman. She disappeared into the tent, returning with a long stick that had hard things on it. She handed it to the man along with a horn and a leather pouch. The man said nothing as he poured something that looked like black sand into the hollow end, pushing it down with a long rod the white boy handed him.

At last the man raised the long stick holding

it with both hands. Thunder roared from the stick's insides! Fire spit from its hollow end. Tree Tall fell back against the tent as a branch cracked away from a tree that grew at the edge of the clearing.

The whiteskin turned toward him with the long stick in his hands. He pointed to it, then to the tree. Then he said the only word Tree Tall had ever heard of the white man's language before today.

"Rifle!"

Rifle. That was what Spotted Elk said had injured his father Gray Seal. Was this whiteskin going to hurt Tree Tall as Gray Seal had been hurt?

3

Jerome—A New Friend

TREE TALL looked up at the white-skinned man holding the long stick he called a rifle. Would the man with the washed-out skin turn the fire-throwing stick on him now? Would Tree Tall snap in two the way the tree branch had? Would he be crippled like Gray Seal?

It seemed forever as the boy waited for the man to do something. The man's woman and the white boy and girl stood watching. At last the man said something to the woman. Tree Tall could not understand the words. But the two seemed to be deciding what to do about the Indian boy who had run into their camp a short time before. Tree Tall held his breath.

The woman nodded at last and picked up another biscuit, handing it to the Indian boy. The white boy then went to a big wooden box

"Tell them we use the rifle only to bring food to our fire," said the man with hair on his face.

that had wheels on all four corners, coming back with a chunk of dried meat. He gave that to Tree Tall, too.

Tree Tall looked up at the man whose hair covered nearly half his face. The man's cheeks crinkled up toward his eyes like he might be smiling behind the face hair. The whiteskin stepped back then motioning for Tree Tall to leave.

The boy moved cautiously, holding the meat and biscuit against him. As he passed the whiteskin the man stopped him. "Tell your people we have the stick that breaks tree branches." He used sign language as he talked so the Indian boy could understand. "Tell them we use the rifle only to bring food to our fire."

The boy nodded, his dark eyes wide with fright. Clutching the food Tree Tall ran as fast as his legs would carry him toward the forest. He continued running up the tree-sheltered path all the way to the top of the hill. At last he stopped. He leaned against a tree breathing in great gulps of air.

The sun was starting to slide down the other side of the sky. He could tell by the sun rays that filtered through the thick tree limbs. His mother would be worried. His grandmother would be angry. His father—well, Gray Seal had probably not even missed him. Since his father had been injured by the whiteskins he paid little attention to Tree Tall. All Gray Seal did was sit and carve pieces of wood. Some he made for Little Pine to use—like the bowls and cooking sticks. Other things were carved into strange-looking creatures that came from Gray Seal's imagination.

After resting, Tree Tall began trotting downhill toward his village. When he reached the clearing he saw his mother talking to Spotted Elk beside their lodge. Little Pine turned as Tree Tall ran out of the forest carrying the meat and biscuit.

"Where have you been?" Little Pine asked with relief. "I have been looking for you." She stopped and looked at the food he carried. "What have you there?"

The boy held the meat out to his mother. "I have been over the hill at the whiteskin's camp. They captured me, but I broke away. I took this food from them, then ran back here with it."

He watched to see if his mother and Spotted Elk were impressed with his lie. Spotted Elk, his wide face set with disbelief, did not look pleased. Neither did Little Pine. Just then his grandmother came out of their cedar plank lodge. His father, Gray Seal, was behind her leaning heavily on the forked pole that helped him walk.

"You lie!" his grandmother spoke with a snap.

Gray Seal shook his head. "So—my son

defeats the whiteskins when his father could not. I am no better than a dead man. I would like to think you lie, Tree Tall. Maybe you stole the meat from one of our own people."

"No. This is not like anything our people have. Here." The boy held out the biscuit. He wished he had told them the truth instead of making himself sound so brave. They might have believed him then.

His grandmother took the biscuit and bit into it as though she thought it might bite her back. "It is not like our food," she admitted, looking closer at the boy. "You tell us again. Only the truth this time."

Tree Tall nodded. "I ran over the hill to see what the whiteskins looked like. I was not careful and stumbled into their camp. The man held me there. He gave me food. Then he took the long stick—the rifle that spits fire—and made a branch break away from a tree at the edge of the forest.

"They gave me this food then and let me go. The whiteskin said to tell my people he has a rifle. He uses it only to bring food to his cooking fire."

Spotted Elk turned to Gray Seal. "You will kill the whiteskins now for what they did to you! Spotted Elk will help. Then the evil spirit may leave and you will walk again."

"No!" Tree Tall exclaimed. The whiteskins did

not hurt me. They gave me food."

Spotted Elk shook his head. "You can be happy the whiteskins did not keep you as their slave. They have taken other Indians to do their work."

Tree Tall knew Gray Seal and Spotted Elk hated the whiteskins. Some had come years before he was born. He had heard Spotted Elk talk of it. The white-skinned trappers brought sickness to the Indians. Many died. Where once their people had been many, now they were few. Spotted Elk's woman had been sick for a long time from an illness she caught from other Indians who had been with the whiteskins.

Gray Seal looked down at his legs. "I cannot fight the whiteskins now."

Later, when it was time for the evening meal, Little Pine cut the dried meat into strips and gave them all some to eat. It tasted different from any they had eaten before.

That night Tree Tall lay on his beaver skin robe in their lodge thinking about the white-skinned people. They had not hurt him. They had given him food. He decided he would go back to visit the whiteskins again.

The next morning Tree Tall took up his spear to go catch more speckled trout. He pulled some vines from a bush and twisted them into a net on his way to his secret fishing rock beside the creek. Soon the boy had four fish in his vine net.

He hid the spear then and carried the fish around the clearing to where the path led over the hill to the clearing on the other side where the whiteskins camped. He slowed to a walk, approaching their tent cautiously.

The white woman and the girl were standing by the fire. Tree Tall walked up to the woman and placed the fish on the ground in front of her.

"So," she said, "you came back. And what have you there? Fish?" She made a sign. "For us?"

Tree Tall nodded.

The white woman's mouth and eyes smiled at him. Nodding her thanks, she picked up the fish and handed them to the girl to clean. Just then the man and boy walked out of the forest from the opposite direction. They, too, seemed glad to see the Indian boy. Soon the white woman had a meal ready and they all sat down on a fallen tree log to eat. The man patted a place between himself and the white boy. Tree Tall sat with them.

The man then put his head forward with his chin close to his chest and spoke words without looking up. The others all put their chins down too. Tree Tall bent down so he could look at their faces. They had their eyes closed. As soon as the man stopped talking, they all looked up smiling. As the woman passed food around they gave Tree Tall a blue-and-white bowl. There was some kind of meat cooked with other things. The meat tasted good, but Tree Tall did not like the rootlike things it was cooked with.

After they had eaten the boy (who was called Jerome) showed Tree Tall the long box with wheels at each corner, saying the word *wagon*. He then took Tree Tall to where the three animals with long fat horns and smooth hide grazed. The white boy called two of them *oxen*. One that was a little different he called a *cow*.

So, Tree Tall thought, that was a cow!

By the time the Indian boy had to leave he had learned many of the whiteskins' words. He showed the pale-skinned boy what some of his words meant, too. As he left the white woman tried to give him something to take back with him. Tree Tall shook his head. He did not want to have to explain where he had been. If he hurried he could be back at the creek in time to spear more trout so he would not have to return to his lodge without any fish. His mother counted on him to bring them their evening meal. Tree Tall knew he had to do his part to help.

The boy speared more trout and was back at their lodge in plenty of time, so he did not get into trouble. He would keep his tongue silent about his visit to the whiteskins. It would only make his grandmother angry, his father sad, and cause his mother to worry.

He would go back to see the whiteskins again. If Spotted Elk was right about the whiteskins taking Indians as slaves, he might find himself in trouble. And yet his urge to know more about these strange people was stronger than his fear.

4

Captured

A MONTH PASSED. Tree Tall had become a regular visitor at the whiteskins' tent lodge. He learned to understand their words. Sometimes he ate with them at midday, since his own family ate only at sunrise and sunset. Each time the white man would put his chin forward on his chest, speaking words before they ate.

One day Tree Tall asked Jerome, "Who father talk before eat?"

Jerome smiled. "He talks to God."

"God?" Tree Tall questioned. "Where this God?"

"Our God is a mighty Spirit. He is everywhere."

Tree Tall nodded. He understood spirits. "We know spirits. Our people come back as the salmon, the elk, the—"

"No," Jerome interrupted. I mean the one, true, all-powerful God who made the earth, the fish, the animals, and men and women. His Son Jesus came to earth long ago. Jesus taught the people to love God, his Father, so he could be our Father, too. Jesus was good. But the people didn't like hearing how they were not pleasing God. So they killed Jesus."

Tree Tall could not understand. "If this God have spirit power, not kill his son!"

"Jesus could have stopped them," Jerome replied. "But he didn't. Instead he died for the bad ways of everyone who would ever come to believe and trust him as God's Son. Then something exciting happened. After dying he came back to life." Jerome hesitated in order to give the Indian boy time to think this through.

Tree Tall's eyes grew wide as the white boy continued. "Later Jesus went to be with God in heaven above where he is now. But he's coming back someday. Until then he sent the Holy Spirit to help us be the kind of people God wants us to be."

To Tree Tall Jerome's words sounded like some of the Indian legends his grandmother told. He felt many legends were probably only make-believe. And yet, the way Jerome talked about Jesus and God his Father, Tree Tall decided these whiteskins must believe their legend to be true.

As time went on Little Pine began to suspect her son was not telling the whole truth about what kept him away from their lodge so much. At last he told his mother when they were alone. He did not want his father or grandmother to know.

Little Pine shook her head. "You could get hurt like your father. Or be taken as their slave so I would never see you again. You are the only son I have. I could not bear to lose you."

"But they are my friends," Tree Tall said.

Little Pine looked doubtful. "I need you to help gather food for the coming days of the long rains. Your father has given up. He will not even try now. I ask much of you, I know. It would be easier for both of us if you had a sister who could help. But there is no sister."

Tree Tall understood Little Pine's longing for a daughter. But he had never heard her speak about his father that way before. He, too, had wondered about Gray Seal. It seemed his pride had been injured even more than his legs.

Little Pine sighed. "You may visit with the whiteskins, but you must spend more time help-ing gather food. We will not talk of the whiteskins to the others."

Soon after this Jerome told Tree Tall he and his family would be leaving the clearing. They were going farther north to a whiteskin's village they called Oregon City. Jerome's father at first had wanted to build a cabin in the clearing and make that their home. But he had changed his mind.

Tree Tall was uncertain of the meaning of some of the white boy's words. But he was too sad to ask. He would miss Jerome. On the day the whiteskins prepared to leave, Tree Tall talked to his friend.

"You come back?"

"I don't know," Jerome replied.

"You—me," the Indian boy pointed first to Jerome and then to himself, "like brothers."

Jerome nodded. "Yes. I've never had a brother before."

"Brothers not go way," Tree Tall pointed out with a down-turn to his mouth.

"Maybe we will see each other again. But if we don't in this life, we can at least be together after we die. That is if you accept Jesus as your Savior. Then we will both go to be with him after death."

Tree Tall's face was questioning. "Sav-ior?"

Jerome seemed to be trying to think of the right words to talk. "If you let Jesus save you from the wrong things you say and do and think, then he will be your Savior. We call those wrong things sin. Jesus died to save us from being punished for our sins by God."

"Oh. Tree Tall have many sin to be saved from." He smiled, then became serious again.

"How Tree Tall get Sav-ior?"

Jerome explained as well as he could to the Indian boy how to become a follower of Christ—a Christian. He wasn't sure Tree Tall understood, but there was so little time before he and his family were to leave the clearing.

Tree Tall was sad for many days after Jerome and his family moved on. Their oxen pulled the wagon away after they covered it with the white canvas of their tent. The cow, whose milk Tree Tall had learned to drink, was tied to the back of the wagon. He stood watching until he could see them no longer.

Afterward, Tree Tall tried talking to Jerome's God so he could one day be with Jerome and Jesus. But the Indian boy did not know the right words to use when he prayed. He wished he knew more about the whiteskins' Great Spirit God and of his Son. Now there was no one to teach him.

One day Spotted Elk came into their village with news. Different whiteskins were camping on the other side of the hill where Jerome's family had been. Tree Tall asked Spotted Elk if it might be the same people.

"These whiteskins," Spotted Elk said, shaking his head, "have heavy traps with sharp teeth that catch the beaver and muskrat. They are called trappers. They kill many animals. More than they use."

The next morning Tree Tall decided to find out if maybe Spotted Elk had been wrong. Maybe it was Jerome's family. He ran up the forest path and down the other side of the hill to the clearing. He watched for a time from behind a tree. Spotted Elk had been right. This was a different whiteskin.

A man sat alone on the fallen tree Jerome's family used to sit on when they ate. Several dead beavers were scattered around him. He was skinning one of them. There were no oxen or cows and no wagon. Four horses grazed in the clearing. The boy looked with longing at the horses. Someday maybe he would have such an animal!

A second man came out of the trees. He carried more dead beavers. This man had hair on his face like Jerome's father. Tree Tall now knew it was called a beard.

Deciding the men looked peaceable, Tree Tall came out of his hiding place and walked across the clearing toward them. The barefaced one looked up. He nudged the other man. The bearded one reached behind him to pick up a rifle. Tree Tall kept walking until he stopped in front of the two men.

"You talk Jesus?" the boy asked.

The men looked at one another. The bearded man rubbed his chin. "Where'd you learn about Jesus? Is there a mission around here?"

"Mission?" There was a question in Tree Tall's voice. "Not know mission."

"Where do you live?" the barefaced man asked, slowly getting to his feet.

Tree Tall motioned over the hill.

"You alone?"

The boy nodded.

The bearded man put his rifle down and bent to pick up a beaver. "Ever skin one of these?"

Tree Tall shook his head. "Father skin beaver. Not boy." He glanced at the other beaver on the ground. There were some hides already drying in the sun. "My people take only what need."

"Want me to teach you to skin a beaver?" the man asked. "Then you'll be able to help your father."

Tree Tall nodded. He reached for the knife the bearded man handed him. It reminded him of a knife he had seen Jerome's father use. He had often thought of how Gray Seal would like to have such a knife to carve the wood.

Tree Tall tried hard to do just as he was told as he began to skin the beaver. The two whiteskins looked at one another and smiled every now and then. The boy decided they must be pleased he was doing such good work.

After awhile he noticed the sun was slipping far down in the sky. It would be evening before long. He had been gone longer than the other times. He put the knife down. "Go now."

"You're not going anywhere," the man declared.

"Wait just a minute!" The barefaced man took hold of the boy's arm. "You haven't finished your job here."

"Go now!" Tree Tall insisted.

"You're not going anywhere," the man declared. "You're staying with us to help skin these beavers." He tightened his grip on the boy's arm until it hurt.

Tree Tall's heart pounded. These men were not anything like Jerome's family. Their eyes had turned hard. Tree Tall thought they killed too many beaver. He looked up into the man's face. Were these the kind of whiteskins who took Indian boys as slaves?

The bearded man went to where their packs lay on the ground while the other man held onto Tree Tall. The one with the hairy face returned with a long chain. The boy had seen short chains on the oxen harness belonging to Jerome's father. The man put one end of the chain around Tree Tall's right ankle, snapping a lock into two links to hold it fast. Then he looped the other end around the log wedging it over a broken limb. The boy was chained like an animal!

He looked longingly toward the forest where the path led back to his village. Would he ever see his mother again? Or Gray Seal? Or his grandmother? At that moment he would have even welcomed a scolding from the sharp-tongued old woman.

44

Night closed in on the clearing. The men talked as they cooked their evening meal, tossing him bits of food as they might feed a dog.

"We better light out of here tonight," the barefaced man said. "That kid's people are liable to come looking for him."

"Naw," the other man said. "They don't care nothin' about their kids. Probably won't even miss him. We'll leave right after daylight."

Tree Tall shivered. They meant to take him away. He was a captive of the whiteskins!

5

Race Against the Rifle

THE bearded white-skinned trapper tossed a blanket over Tree Tall before the two men lay down on the other side of the fire. The boy tried again and again to pull the locked chain off over his foot. But it was too tight.

He thought of his mother and father. He thought of his grandmother. They would be worried. They might guess where he had gone, since Little Pine knew he had often visited the other whiteskins. What if the men of his village came led by Spotted Elk? They could not stand against the whiteskins' rifles.

The boy thought of Jerome, too. He was sure if Jerome's father knew what these white-skinned trappers had done he would make them let him go.

Thinking of Jerome made him remember the

whiteskins' God and his Son Jesus. Jerome had said he could pray—talk to God, the Great Spirit—and ask for help. But would the God of whiteskins listen to an Indian boy? Especially when he asked for help to escape from whiteskins? Tree Tall was not sure. And yet, if the Great Spirit God knew how these trappers had treated him, maybe he would help. The boy noticed the two men had not talked in prayer before eating as Jerome's father had. Maybe they did not know Jesus. Maybe they did not know of the Great Spirit God at all.

There was something Jerome said Tree Tall needed to ask first, before he could be a Jesus person. What was it? "I know," Tree Tall whispered to himself. "I must ask God to forgive those things I do wrong. Because Jesus died to bring all who believe into God's family."

The boy lay there for a time just thinking. It made sense. He had done lots of wrong things. There was something inside him that caused him to lie. Sometimes he stole from others. He did lots of things he was told not to do. He should not have come here!

Tree Tall closed his eyes there in the darkness and began to talk to God in his own language. Then he stopped. Maybe the Great Spirit God knew only the words of the whiteskin. Tree Tall did not know what to do. At last he began again using the same halting words as when he talked

47

to Jerome. He told God how bad he had been. It nearly broke Tree Tall's heart to remember some of the things he had done. He asked God to forgive him—to let Jesus clean out the bad of his heart and to watch over him and help him now.

The boy lay there for a long time. He had stopped trying to pull the chain off his leg. "Jesus, help me get away. Help me get to village," Tree Tall whispered. He was so tired. With that said, he slept.

Tree Tall awoke as day was about to dawn. He lay there without moving. He was still chained to the log. But for some reason he felt as free as the sea birds that floated on wide wings over the salt waters. Something happy lay with lightness on his heart.

Looking up at the stars that were growing dim as the sky turned lighter, Tree Tall whispered aloud, "Tree Tall of Jesus' family. Clean inside. Tree Tall say, thank to Great Spirit God. Know now, Jesus die even for Indian boy here in land of long rains!"

One of the men moved beyond the fire. "You say somethin'?" he asked the other.

"No. Probably that Indian kid chantin' to himself."

The bearded one got up to check on the boy. Tree Tall's ankle throbbed where he had tried to pull the chain over his foot the night before.

"Hurt," he complained to the man.

The white trapper, without a word, unlocked the chain and put it around the other leg. He then went back to stir up the fire.

Tree Tall sat up rubbing his freed ankle. It felt good having the chain off that leg. As he moved he felt the chain pull loose from his other ankle. He moved again. Then, cautiously pulling the edge of the blanket back, he saw the chain had fallen off. The man had carelessly not locked it. He was free!

Moving noiselessly Tree Tall watched the whiteskins by the fire as he bunched the blanket together so it would look like he was still lying underneath it. He rolled away then, crawling around the end of the log. The boy stopped to look over the top to see if the men had noticed him. They had not. He began crawling away. The horses snorted as he crept past them. Maybe he could ride one of the horses. But how would he get onto its back? They were so tall.

"What's wrong with those horses?" one man asked the other.

The second man's voice showed irritation. "I don't know. Go check on them."

Tree Tall knew it was now or never. He had no time to try to take a horse. He jumped up and ran toward the trees.

Behind him he heard a shout. "Hey! It's the kid. He's gettin' away. Here, hand me my rifle.

49

It's already loaded."

Tree Tall was running as fast as he could. A few more strides and he would be in the forest. He would be safe. His ankle hurt. But there was no time to think of that now.

He heard a click from behind. Then. . . .

Boom!

The rifle spoke, sending lead singing past without touching him. It had missed. He ran on, reaching the trees at last. Behind one of the men yelled. "Take my rifle. Aim this time. We don't want him gettin' away and bringin' his whole tribe down on us."

Another roar thundered behind Tree Tall as the second rifle spoke. The boy dodged to the right as lead thudded into a tree beside him. The rifle had missed again. He ran wild, dodging trees and brush as he circled back to the trail that led to his village. He had outrun the rifle of the whiteskins!

At the top of the hill he stopped to rest. His chest hurt from breathing so hard. After lying chained to the log all night, his legs felt like limp fish. At last he recovered enough to start on again. He took off at his easy trot.

Tree Tall thought about Jesus and his Father, God, to whom he had prayed the night before. He glanced up through the branches of the trees. The morning was clothed in mist. The sun and blue sky were hidden from view. But he knew they were there beyond the mist, just as he knew the Great Spirit God and his Son Jesus were with him and had helped him escape from the whiteskins.

Jerome had been right. God does care and help those who love him. Tree Tall felt such love at that moment. It was almost more than he could bear. "Thank, God," he spoke with Jerome's words. "Thank, Jesus."

When Tree Tall came breathlessly into the clearing of his village he found the men standing in front of his lodge. Spotted Elk was there with his hunting bow and long spear. They were talking excitedly. He heard Spotted Elk say, "I heard the sound of the long stick. It came from over the hill. It—"

Spotted Elk stopped as Tree Tall ran by, throwing himself into the arms of his grandmother—the first member of his family he saw.

She held him against her for a few seconds, then pushed him back to look at him, her hand on one hip. "Are you all right, boy?"

Tree Tall nodded. "The whiteskins chained me to a log. They were going to take me away to be their slave, to skin the beaver for them. I got loose and ran. They fired their rifles at me."

Spotted Elk nodded. "I heard the long sticks. It did not strike you?"

The boy shook his head. He was glad they believed him this time. Grownups seemed to

51

know when truth was spoken.

Little Pine and Gray Seal came toward him. "Are you hurt?" Little Pine asked.

"No, the great God protected me." They all listened as the boy told what had happened. He showed them his ankle where the chain had rubbed into the skin turning it an angry red. When he finished his story, he looked at Gray Seal. His father spoke not one word.

Spotted Elk took two of the men and went back the way Tree Tall had come, making sure the whiteskins had not followed him to their village. When they returned they said the white-skinned trappers had left, taking their beaver pelts with them.

For a time Tree Tall was content to stay close to his village. The days passed. The leaves fell from the willow trees along the creek bank. The wind turned crisp until at last the rain began to fall. Tree Tall's people usually left their village during the days of the warm sun to go higher in the mountains to gather food. They returned again when the leaves dropped from the big-leafed trees. But this time they had decided to stay where they were. The salt waters were close by with clams and bird eggs. The creek was full of fish. Berries grew in the woods and food roots in the ground. There were more and more whiteskins everywhere. So far none had come to their village. They felt safe here.

Besides, it would be difficult for Gray Seal to go far now.

The mountains were close where the men hunted for deer and elk. They had caught and dried many salmon earlier. Spotted Elk shared some of his meat with Gray Seal's family. In return, Little Pine made beautiful baskets for Spotted Elk's woman since she was still too sick to do much work. Little Pine gave them berries, too, and shared roots she and Tree Tall dug.

Gray Seal walked a little now, using the forked pole to support himself. He carved wooden bowls and cooking sticks for Spotted Elk's lodge, taking pride in the beauty of the wood and what he could make. Tree Tall had never seen such lovely bowls before. He was learning to be proud of his father's carvings. He just wished Gray Seal would talk more.

As the long rains came, the people of his village settled down to a less busy life. It was time to eat the food they had gathered and dried during the warmer days. The women made baskets for their own use and for trading. The men, except for Gray Seal, spent some of their days making canoes from cedar trees they felled by setting fire to the trunks and burning them through. They controlled the fire by packing wet sand around the tree.

They did not live on a river, as most of the Indians in that region. Because of this their canoes had to be large enough to cross the salt rolls of the big waters so they could paddle up the land-line to where the many rivers flowed out to mingle with those of salt.

There, when the days grew warm, they would paddle upriver to the salmon-catching places and camp beside the other Indians. They would trade their baskets, extra canoes, and fur skins for other things they could use.

Tree Tall looked forward to those times. For then there would be other children to spend time with. Sometimes he was lonely with only the older people to talk to.

Another thing Tree Tall enjoyed were the times of the rainy day festivals. Those of his tribe came from other villages or else his family went to theirs. The shamans did their medicine dances and called on the good spirits. Presents were given and everyone was happy. But now—since Gray Seal had been hurt—Tree Tall's family could not journey away from their village as before. And since Gray Seal did not go, few came to their lodge.

Next year, when Tree Tall was ready to become a man, he would be sent alone into the forest for several days during the times of the warm sun. He would then wait to tell everyone at a rainy day festival about the spirit who had visited him to become his lifelong guardian.

The boy wondered what his family would say

Tree Tall did not know it at that moment, but his world was about to change forever.

if he told them he was thinking of asking Jesus, the Son of the Great Spirit God, to be his guardian? He decided he had better not tell them just yet. They did not know of this Jesus.

Besides, it was not the usual way for the Indian boy to choose his own guardian. The spirit was supposed to choose the boy. But his father did not have presents to give to those who would come to such a festival to celebrate Tree Tall's manhood. Because of this, the boy decided it would probably be just as well for him to go ahead and seek the whiteskin's God as his guardian. He saw no reason to wait until he was another year older.

The weather at last grew warm again. Buds began to swell into leaves at the ends of the willow branches. The deer would soon be grazing with their spotted fawns in the meadows. Life seemed good again to Tree Tall.

Then one day there came the sound of hoof-beats on the path that led down from the hill behind their village. It was the rumble of many hooves. Spotted Elk and the other men—except for Gray Seal—ran for their bows and spears as white-skinned men rode out of the trees and into the clearing. They sat straight on sleek spirited horses.

Tree Tall did not know it at that moment, but his world was about to change forever. The old ways would never be the same again.

6

On the Trail of Good-Bye

TREE TALL heard a jangling sound, too, like the clank of many chains as twelve mounted whiteskins rode into his village. These whiteskins were the first to reach their village. They wore clothes all the same, the color of the huckleberry. There were bright shiny sunlike spots down the front of their shirts. The men sat astride sleek, long-legged horses. Tree Tall later learned that these were cavalry men, soldiers of the whiteskins.

Spotted Elk, who knew Tree Tall could talk with the strange words, took the boy with him to meet the head whiteskin. Tree Tall faced the man on the horse as the soldier spoke.

"Does anyone here speak English?"

The boy stepped forward. "Tree Tall talk. Not know . . . En-lish."

The man smiled below the thick hair that grew on his upper lip. "Tell your people a treaty has been signed by your tribe. The white man is giving the Indians land to live on just north of here. You will all be given food and clothes. Everything you need will be there. The Indians have been troubling my people. Now they must go live where the white soldiers can be sure they will not harm white settlers."

Tree Tall told Spotted Elk as much as he understood of the whiteskin's words. Spotted Elk listened, then declared they had not harmed any white settlers. Spotted Elk added, "The land is not the whiteskins' to give. It is ours. All of it!"

The boy spoke Spotted Elk's words to the white soldier. The man nodded. "You must still move onto the reservation with the others."

Spotted Elk became very angry. "No!" he shouted, raising his arm over his head as though striking out at the clouds above. "We will not leave our village. Tell him we have harmed no one!"

The boy related Spotted Elk's words to the whiteskin again. Suddenly the white soldiers began pulling out their rifles from where they carried the long stick on their saddles. They moved their horses forward, positioning themselves beside all five lodges.

Spotted Elk looked worried. He called the

"You must still move onto the reservation with the others," the
soldier said.

men of the village together. He noted they had no rifles to fight the whiteskins. They would die if they tried to resist. At last Spotted Elk told Tree Tall to tell the whiteskin that they would go just as soon as they packed their belongings.

The head white soldier nodded. "Good. We will be back this time tomorrow to take you all to the reservation."

By the next day Tree Tall's mother and grandmother had everything packed that they could carry. Gray Seal sat sullen ... watching. Tree Tall was worried about his father. Would he be able to walk?

There were more white soldiers when they returned. Some led pack horses. The head one told Tree Tall how much better off they would be on the reservation. He said they would be given everything they needed. They would never have to hunt or fish again. It made the boy sad. Did the whiteskin not know hunting was a part of the Indian's life? And what about their freedom? Tree Tall's family had always gone where they wanted—when they wanted to go. But, of course, that was before Gray Seal had been hurt by the whiteskins.

The soldiers strapped the Indian's possessions on the pack horses. When the Indian people were ready, three soldiers led the way, sitting straight and tall on their horses' backs. The column of Indians walked behind, the women carrying food in their cooking baskets for the journey. Spotted Elk's woman had been placed on a horse led by a soldier who followed behind with the rest of the white-skinned men.

Tree Tall looked back at the cedar lodge his father had built. He looked toward the creek where he had caught the fat trout to help feed his family. Would he ever see this place—his home—again?

Gray Seal struggled along using his forked pole to help him walk. They had not gone far when one of the soldiers offered Gray Seal a packhorse to ride. Gray Seal ignored the white soldier. He would walk, he told Tree Tall.

For the first time in months Tree Tall saw a spark of life in his father's eyes. The boy decided that was good. And yet, it would not help his father's legs to walk the long miles before them.

At last Gray Seal gave out and nearly fell. Without a word Spotted Elk came back and boosted his friend up on the offered horse. Tree Tall tried not to look into his father's eyes after that.

They stopped and made camp that first night. The soldiers camped close by the Indians. The next day they started on again, coming to another Indian village. These, too, were packed and ready to move against their will to the reservation where they were all to live. Never again would they be able to move their villages wherever they wanted, or to go to the mountains to hunt as before. They would have only the reservation land now.

When they reached the reservation that evening they found those who had arrived earlier had already chosen the best locations to build their lodges. There was much confusion. While some were building lodges, others were camping in the open place by the river. Tree Tall and his people were looked down on, since their village was so small. Several tribes were gathered here. Some had been enemies for many years. They had strange ways, unknown to Tree Tall. In fact, some of the other Indians were as frightening to Tree Tall's people as the whiteskins.

Tree Tall gathered fir branches from nearby trees and helped his family put up a lean-to shelter until they could build a lodge. Little Pine said she was glad it was spring. At least they had not been forced to move during the cold rainy days.

A week crept by. Tree Tall's people stayed close together. Spotted Elk had also put up only a lean-to. He seemed to be watching all that was happening ... waiting. Whenever Tree Tall wandered through camp some of the other boys, from a different tribe, called him names he did not understand. Even their words were unknown to him.

One day Tree Tall could stand it no longer. He

picked up a stick as though to hit them. But they pulled the stick away, knocking him to the ground. Three boys piled on top of him. When it was over, Tree Tall's face and arms were scratched.

That night he did something he had forgotten to do for the past several days. He prayed to Jesus for help. For some reason it did not make him feel better, as it had before. Then he realized he was angry. He was angry at the whiteskins, and at his father and Spotted Elk for not standing up to them. He was angry at the other Indians who made his life miserable. He was even angry at Jesus for letting this terrible thing happen in the first place.

The days dragged on. The weather grew warmer. Life on the reservation did not get any better. The white soldiers brought scrawny cows for the Indians to kill and eat. The meat was tough and tasteless—not like the wild deer or elk.

The soldiers brought clothes of the whiteskins, too, telling the Indian people they must now cover their bodies with the strange cloth. Tree Tall and his family had never before felt shame for their red-brown skin. In warm weather it was their custom to wear very little. But the head white soldier said they must now wear the whiteskins' clothes or else they would be given no food from the scrawny cows.

Tree Tall looked through a pile of clothing. Most were patched or had holes in them. He started to turn away. He would not wear the whiteskins' throwaways!

But his mother stopped him. "We must eat," Little Pine spoke, handing him a pair of baggy brown pants and a scratchy shirt with holes at both elbows. "You will put these on." There was no hint of a possibility of talking his way out of doing as told.

Little Pine picked out two dresses from another pile, then she found a shirt and pants for Gray Seal. Tree Tall's grandmother glared at Little Pine as she carried the things back to their lean-to followed by Tree Tall.

"I will not put on the skins of the whites!" the old woman hissed.

"Yes," her daughter spoke softly. "You will wear this." She handed the dress to her mother. "And you will keep it on. We will eat. We will not starve. We will live."

Tree Tall's grandmother jerked the dress out of Little Pine's hands and yanked it on over her head, standing there with her arms out from her sides. "There! Does this make my daughter happy? Does this make an old Indian woman into an old white-skinned woman?"

Little Pine turned away—but not before Tree Tall saw a tear escape her eye. He had never seen his mother cry before.

Gray Seal refused the shirt and pants Little Pine placed in front of him, retreating into the lean-to out of sight.

Little Pine then turned to Tree Tall. He sighed, struggling into the too-big pants and the too-small shirt. He felt all tied up inside them. They made him itch. But he tried not to show his feelings to his mother, realizing she was doing only what she felt she had to do.

Two days later more soldiers came. They told the Indians to stand in line in front of a table. One by one they were made to walk up and do something they called "register." Each was given a new name—a whiteskin's name. They were told they should learn to speak the whiteskins' language. Then the tribes would all speak with the same words and become one people—one tribe. They were told it would be better to put away their old ways and words and now speak what the whiteskins called English.

Spotted Elk was in line just in front of Tree Tall and his family. The boy heard a soldier say, "You will be called Charlie Johns." Spotted Elk stared down at the whiteskin. Finally he made a mark on the paper before him, then stalked away.

"And you shall be Matthew Stone, young man," the soldier said to Tree Tall. "Is this your family?"

The boy nodded.

One by one the soldier gave new names to his parents and grandmother. Little Pine was to be Mary Stone. Gray Seal was named Jim Stone. And Tree Tall's grandmother was to be Lilly Smith. Each marked the paper and then went back to their lean-to.

Tree Tall thought his heart would break. His people were being treated like children. He had seen the long rains twelve times since he had been born. He wished it had been more and he was bigger. He would then fight the whiteskins and the bad Indians. He tried praying, but his heart was filled with too much anger.

As the moon again reached its fullness Tree Tall realized he had all he could stand of the reservation. Little Pine (he would always call her that no matter what the whiteskins said he must call her) was sad all the time. She had even stopped talking about her longing for a daughter.

Gray Seal continued to nurse his own thoughts in silence. Only his grandmother seemed to have courage left in her. For the first time Tree Tall felt very close to his grandmother. He decided they were much alike.

One night when the moon was still full and bright the boy raised up from his beaver-skin robe and crept out of the lean-to. He found some dried meat and a blanket the whiteskins had given them. He took a fire-making stick his people used to twirl between their hands so fast sparks would catch fire to dry slivers of wood. He found the loin-piece he had worn. He rolled it, the meat, and the fire stick inside the blanket.

Then he softly walked through the camp of sleeping Indians. He did not know where he was going. Nor did he care. He never wanted to return. Never! Anything would be better than living on the reservation with all these strange people and the ever-present white-skinned soldiers.

The boy followed a path that led up the river. When he was far enough away not to be detected, he took off his clothes. Joyfully he tied them to a big rock and threw them in the river. He put his loin-piece on then, tucked the blanket roll under one arm, and broke into his tireless trot. On and on he ran, following the course of the river on a path first made by the animals, deepened by the Indians, and now widened by the white soldiers.

After a time he stopped to rest. The moon shone down, bathing trees and rocks in a crisp veiled light. Ripples glistened on the river's surface. Tree Tall stood looking down at the dark waters that reflected the moon high overhead.

He was sad. What was he going to do? Where would he go? Once again he thought of Jerome.

7

Tree Tall and Bright Sky

TREE TALL stood there beside the moon-bathed river. He was tired. He had not slept since the night before. The reservation was now far behind. He decided he would sleep for a while. Maybe he would know what to do in the morning.

The boy lay down behind a fallen tree well off the path. He pulled the blanket over him and looked up at the moon high overhead. He thought about his mother and father. He thought about his grandmother. Then he thought about Jesus.

Why had Jesus and his Father, God the Great Spirit, allowed Tree Tall's people to be taken to the reservation? Why did God not release them the way he had released the chain from Tree Tall's leg when the trappers captured him?

"Do you hear me, Jesus?" the boy prayed aloud in his own words. "Do you see? Do you care for Tree Tall and Tree Tall's father, mother, grandmother? Help Tree Tall. Help family."

He remembered then the words Jerome said he should add to his prayers. Oh, but it would be so much easier to pray in his own words. If he could just be sure the Great Father could understand. "Tree Tall ask, Jesus' name. You, Jesus, die for Tree Tall. Tree Tall thank."

The boy slept then. It was morning when he awoke. He ate some of the dried beef, then rolled up the blanket again, and started on toward the rising sun. He still was not sure where he was going. He wondered if he could find Oregon City, where Jerome and his family had gone.

Tree Tall had no idea where to look other than Jerome had pointed in the same direction the wild geese flew when the sun warmed the earth. That would make it not only the way of the geese, but a little off toward the rising sun from where Tree Tall was now.

He followed along the river until it became narrow. At last it disappeared. The trees grew thicker as the path led continually up toward the high mountain that rose before him. The day promised to be warm. Tree Tall was glad not to be wearing the whiteskins' clothes. He walked all day, stopping to eat and sleep only when the sun went down.

Two days passed. The boy had crossed the mountain following the trail. He had seen no one since leaving the reservation. He was beginning to feel so alone.

That evening, just as he was about to stop for the night, he came upon a clearing. A creek flowed nearby. It looked like a good place to make a spear and catch some trout. It would taste good again after eating the whiteskins' food.

He left the trail and started across the clearing. Then he stopped. Something had happened here not long before. The tall grass was all mashed down in places. A horse lay dead off to one side, an arrow in its side. Arrows were all about. He found a broken hunting bow, too.

"Maybe," he spoke to himself, "maybe Indians left the reservation. Or maybe these are from Indians who have not yet been gathered by the white soldiers."

As he stood there looking around he heard a sound. Cautiously he walked toward the brush from where the sound had come. He parted the branches and looked in. There lay a small Indian girl. She appeared to be about nine or ten years old. She was dressed in a buckskin garment and moccasins in the manner of a tribe on the dry side of the farther-still mountains toward the rising sun. The tribes from there used to raid Tree Tall's people from time to time.

Tree Tall spoke to her. "You may not understand my words, but I won't hurt you."

She moved her head to look at him. "Who are you?" she asked.

Tree Tall was surprised to hear her speak with his words. "I am Tree Tall. Where did you come from?"

"I am Bright Sky. I was left here after a battle with an enemy tribe. I—I am so hungry. Do you have food?"

The boy lay his blanket roll down and took out what was left of his dried beef. He pushed the brush aside and handed the beef to the girl. She took the meat and ate hungrily. She did not appear hurt, just dirty and hungry. He decided he would make camp down by the creek and spear some fish. She would need more food and he had to eat.

The girl followed him down to the water. While he broke a slender branch from a tree and sharpened one end to a point with a thin stone, the girl washed herself at the water's edge.

"Don't scare the fish," Tree Tall cautioned. He noticed she looked much better clean.

She followed him upstream to a deep pool. Soon the boy had six fat trout roasting on fresh green sticks over the fire he had started with his fire-twirling stick. They ate, then Tree Tall asked where she had come from and how she was able to speak with his words.

Her small moon-shaped face brightened with a snap of her dark eyes as she talked. "My mother and father died of the white man's sickness two long rains ago. I was then sold to another tribe—one that had been an enemy of my people."

"We must come from the same tribe," Tree Tall noted.

"We must," said Bright Sky. "It is good to hear my own words spoken again."

Tree Tall looked around. "What happened here? It looks like there was a battle."

The girl nodded. "When the tribe I was with was attacked, the people ran off leaving me behind. I hid in the brush. They left their village after the white soldiers said they had to go live on land they call a reservation."

"The white soldiers took my people to a reservation, too, toward the going down of the sun," Tree Tall noted.

"We were to go to one on the other side of the far mountains where the sun greets each day." She pointed in the opposite direction from where Tree Tall had just come. "Is it as good on reservation land as the white men said it would be? I wanted to go there, but the tribe I lived with did not trust the white soldiers."

"They were right in not trusting," Tree Tall

replied. "It is not good there. The soldiers make us wear old clothes thrown away by their own people. The good food they promised was old cows about to die. They changed our names to ones of the whiteskins. They make us live together with other tribes who have been at war with us since time began. The whiteskins—" Tree Tall stopped. The girl was laughing.

"What is funny?" he asked.

"You call them whiteskins. They call us redskins. I think both you and the white men forget we are more than skin. We are men and women—boys and girls."

"How do you know so much about the whiteskins? I mean, about the white men?"

"The tribe I lived with traded with white men. I have been many times to their log cabins. I have learned their language."

Tree Tall threw his shoulders back. "I, too, know their words. Jerome, a white boy, is my friend. I now pray to their God."

Bright Sky at last grew tired. Tree Tall let her use his blanket. He gathered some dead tree limbs and piled them next to his fire, adding more just before lying down to keep the night chill from his nearly bare body.

The next morning they ate more fish speared from the creek. Tree Tall roasted four extras, wrapping them in willow leaves to carry. He said, "It is time we left here. I am going toward

73

where the wild geese fly when the earth warms. You will come with me." It was not a question, but a command.

The girl nodded.

They walked all day, stopping that night to eat what was left of the morning's fish. The next day they started on again. They had not walked far when they saw smoke. It was a narrow column like the smoke that rises from a campfire. Tree Tall grew cautious. If the campfire was that of warlike Indians they could be facing trouble. Or maybe they were bad whiteskins.

The boy and girl climbed a low hill to see what was on the other side.

"There's a lodge down there," Tree Tall said. "It's made of whole round trees, not from the long slices of wood split from fallen cedar trees the way we build our lodges."

Bright Sky crawled up beside him. Below them in a meadow was a building of the white settlers. Cows grazed close by. A man walked behind two oxen that pulled something that cut into a patch of cleared ground and turned the earth upside down.

"That's a log cabin," said Bright Sky. "White men build such cabins. The man is plowing the ground." She started to get to her feet. "Let's go down and see if they will give us food."

"No!" The boy pulled her back down beside

him. "I will get food for you soon," he promised. "We will go around their lodge so they do not see us."

"It's a cabin," Bright Sky corrected. "They call it a log cabin."

"You are like all girls. You think you know everything," Tree Tall said with a pout.

"I think I know more about the white men than you who boasts of a white friend and of prayers to their unseen God," she answered sharply.

Tree Tall was beginning to wish he had not found this sharp-tongued girl. She irritated him.

Just then they heard something. It was the sound of horses. Tree Tall would always remember that sound. It reminded him of the time the white soldiers rode into their village to take them away to the reservation.

He grabbed Bright Sky's arm. "Come. We must run. Fast!"

8

Oregon City

TREE TALL ran down the hill dragging Bright Sky by the hand after him. They stopped at the bottom.

Just as they were safely hidden in a clump of bushes, a small company of white soldiers rode their horses two abreast around the bend of the trail Tree Tall had been following. The soldiers were headed in the direction of the cabin on the other side of the hill.

The boy looked at Bright Sky and whispered, "And you wanted to go to the cabin! You are not so bright after all. The soldiers would take us both to the reservation."

As soon as the white soldiers were out of sight, the boy and girl started on. "I'm hungry," complained Bright Sky.

"You are always hungry," said Tree Tall. "We

"The soldiers would take both of us to the reservation," Tree Tall said.

will stop as soon as we come to a creek where I can spear fish."

It was much later, almost sunset, when they finally came to a shallow creek. Long sleek trout moved tapered bodies with a gentle swaying motion beneath a tree that had fallen over the bank. The dark hole under the water was thick with fish. Soon Bright Sky and Tree Tall were roasting their meal, waiting with impatience for the fish to cook over their fire on green sticks.

Afterward Tree Tall asked, "Have you heard of the whiteskins'—I mean, of the white man's village? The one called Oregon City?"

The girl nodded. "It is on the river where the water falls fast over high rocks."

"Have you ever been there?"

She shook her head. "I have only heard of it. There are many wonders there our people have never seen. Some white men who live there come from a place far over the salt waters called England. Others come from the land toward the sunrise. They call themselves Americans. Is that where we are going?"

Tree Tall nodded. "I think it is. But how do you know all of this?"

The girl giggled. "I am not dumb like an Indian boy I know. My name is Bright Sky. Right?"

Tree Tall ignored the girl. He knew she was joking. But he was getting tired of her putting him down all the time.

The next day the two walked on. By afternoon they reached a wide fast-flowing river.

"The tribe I was with caught salmon near here," said Bright Sky. "They dried them over many fires for the winter."

"My people caught the red-fleshed salmon, too," Tree Tall said. "It was in a river many walks from here."

The two followed the river looking for a way to cross. At last they came to a place where the water ran slow and deep around a sharp bend. Tree Tall stopped. A log had drifted downstream. It was lodged between two rocks by the shore. Broken limbs stuck out at odd angles from its slender trunk.

"Can you swim?" Tree Tall asked Bright Sky.

She shook her head.

"Would you be afraid to float across the river on that log." He looked closely at the girl.

"Of course not!" Bright Sky answered. But she looked frightened."

Tree Tall went down to the water's edge, wading in to push the log away from the rocks and toward shore. "Take your moccasins off and sit on the log like you are riding a horse. You can hang on to a broken branch. I'll swim and push you across to the other side."

Bright Sky hesitated.

"Here," he told her. "Get on. You can hold the blanket roll and your moccasins so they won't get wet. If you sit very still the log won't roll with you."

Tree Tall was glad he was not bothered by the whiteskins' clothes now as he pushed the log with Bright Sky astraddle out into the river's current. Hanging on to keep the girl from rolling into the river, Tree Tall kicked his legs hard trying to steer the log toward the opposite bank. But the water moved too fast. All he could do was hang on to keep Bright Sky from falling off.

They seemed to drift for a long time before the river turned another sweeping bend. Tree Tall kicked harder. Slowly the log eased toward the far bank. Just when all appeared to be going the way Tree Tall wanted, the log rolled, pitching Bright Sky into the deep water! The boy let go of the log to grab her. But she was gone!

"Bright Sky!" he screamed into the silence that brooded over the still water.

The log floated on by. Tree Tall treaded water turning this way and that, looking for some sign of the girl.

Floosh!

He turned again to see Bright Sky's hair break through to the water's surface. Her eyes were wide with fright. Tree Tall grabbed for her, tangling his fingers in her hair. She struggled, gasping for air before starting to sink again. Tree Tall hung on, swimming as hard as he could toward the shore. He was so tired he

80

could hardly drag his body out of the water, let alone the thrashing girl. At last they were both on the riverbank. Bright Sky was coughing up water. But she was alive!

She turned to Tree Tall, who lay breathing in great gulps of air beside her. "You—would make—good fish, Indian boy."

The blanket roll was gone now. Somehow she had managed to hang onto her moccasins through it all. But there was no fire-twirling stick. The girl's buckskin garment was heavy with water. But at least the sun was warm.

"They will dry in time," she told Tree Tall, pulling the soaked moccasins on her feet when they were both rested at last.

They started on again, following the river until they stopped for the night. Tree Tall and the girl found some roots, eating them raw for their evening meal. Then he gathered fir branches to cover them for their night's sleep.

The next day they again followed the river until steep cliffs rose close to the bank forming a ledge far above. Climbing to the top they kept the river in view as they continued downstream. The ground finally sloped back to the water's edge for a time. Up ahead they could hear the crashing roar of a waterfall.

Suddenly a piercing whine cut the air. Tree Tall and Bright Sky stopped, falling back a step. "What was that?" the boy wondered aloud.

81

Bright Sky was trembling. "I—I think it might ... might be what they call a sawmill," she said. "I have heard of the terrible noise the saw makes as it rips logs into boards they build their houses with in Oregon City. They use the push of the water falling to turn the saw."

Tree Tall could see fear in the girl's eyes. He was glad. For there was fear inside him, too. The sound rang through the stillness again. It came from just around the bend. "Come," he said. "I would like to see this sawmill."

It was then a voice came from behind them. "Well, where'd you two come from?"

Tree Tall whirled around. There, behind them, was a tall mean-looking white man. Tree Tall grabbed Bright Sky's hand and pulled her forward. Together they ran. There was no place to go but straight ahead. The river blocked them on one side and the high rocky cliffs on the other. As they rounded a bend they saw the houses of the white man's village of Oregon City before them.

A wide path separated two rows of buildings made of flat boards colored white like the snow. There were some horses and wagons, too. Down the center of the dusty path the two children ran. Tree Tall turned to look back to see if the white man was following when he collided with something—with someone! The boy looked up.

"Whoa, there you two," a white man said,

82

reaching out to keep them from falling. "Well, if it isn't Tree Tall! How did you ever get clear up here?"

The boy stared at the man. It was Jerome's father! The Indian boy stopped to catch his breath. "Soldiers come. Take Indian people to reservation. Bad there."

"And who do you have with you?" the man asked. "Is this your sister?"

The boy shook his head. "Have no sister. No brother. Tree Tall find girl. Her mother, father dead. Tribe she with go way, leave her, after fight with other Indians."

The white man frowned, looking closer at Bright Sky. "Are you all right? Were you hurt?"

The girl shook her head but said nothing. Tree Tall smiled inside himself. For once Bright Sky had lost her know-it-all tongue.

The man turned back to Tree Tall. "What do you plan to do?"

Standing taller, the boy answered, "Grow strong. Go back, take mother, father, grandmother away from reservation. No more white man's throwaways."

"And what will you do in the meantime?" the man asked. "Won't your father and mother be even more unhappy on the reservation with their only son gone?"

Tree Tall shrugged his shoulders looking down at his bare toes.

"Tell you what," said the man. "Come home with me as soon as I close my store. Jerome will be glad to see you, I know. We can talk more about what might be best for you later."

The boy hesitated. He looked at Bright Sky. "Girl have no one. No place."

The man smiled. "She can come with us."

He turned and led the way past other white people to a building that held all sorts of things inside. There was food in barrels, knives, axes, and things Tree Tall had never seen before. People came and went, eyeing the Indian children curiously.

They all wore many clothes on their bodies. Even on such a warm day. It seemed strange to the Indian boy. He glanced down at his own bare body covered only by the loin-piece of elk hide. Never before had he known such shame— but suddenly he felt out of place. These whiteskins hid everything but their heads and their hands. Maybe he should not have thrown his pants and shirt away after all. And yet, could he have saved Bright Sky from the river if he had been burdened by so many clothes?

Bright Sky told the boy what many of the things were in the store and how they were used. There were heavy iron pots for cooking like he had seen Jerome's mother using over their campfire. But as fascinating as everything was, Tree Tall decided none compared with the beautiful wooden bowls his father, Gray Seal, carved. Or with the woven baskets his mother made and cooked in.

There was footwear Bright Sky called boots and shoes. They were made of heavy leather. Tree Tall's people went barefoot. He glanced at the soft beaded moccasins Bright Sky wore that had been made by the enemy tribe from across the far mountains. He wondered why the white people tied their feet up in such things as boots and shoes, or else why they did not put more beauty into their things as the Indians did with their moccasins. He felt a little sorry for the whites.

At last the man told the boy and girl it was time to "close the store and go home." Tree Tall and Bright Sky walked with him past a group of white boys to a far building. The pale-skinned boys stared at Tree Tall. He had a feeling they might have tried to run him off if Jerome's father had not been with him, the way the Indian boys had done on the reservation.

"Your cabin?" Tree Tall asked as they reached a high snow-colored building.

"We call this a house," the man explained. "It has two floors, one on top of the other. The sleeping rooms are all upstairs. You've probably never seen a house like this painted white."

Tree Tall shook his head.

"This is the kind of house my people live in

back in the Eastern towns," the man said.

"Many whiteskins—white people—there?" the boy questioned, glancing quickly at Bright Sky.

"Yes," the man said. "Many, many more.

"Why leave? You not miss old home?"

The man stopped, looking down at the boy. "Yes, I do miss it at times. You're thinking about your old home, aren't you? And of how you would like to go back?"

Tree Tall nodded. "We same. Away from old homes. Tree Tall and his people cannot go back to village to live. White soldiers not let."

There was a sadness reflected in the man's eyes. "I know. That's why we both need to do the best we can to make our new homes good. Come. We'll talk more later, after we've had supper."

The three walked up to the house together. Tree Tall and Bright Sky waited as the man opened the door. He motioned for them to go in ahead of him.

Bright Sky hung back as Tree Tall stepped in through the open door. He caught his breath. He had no idea white people lived in such a way. Then he saw it! A chill raced through him.

Over the fire pit, on wooden pegs, was the long stick—the white man's rifle. No matter where he went Tree Tall seemed forever to be brought under the power of the fire-throwing stick.

9

Back to the Reservation

INSIDE the white man's house Tree Tall and Bright Sky found many new and strange things besides the dreaded rifle on the wall. Former fires had blackened the enclosed fire pit that was built next to a wall under the rifle.

The white man had made his fire pit out of a hollowed-out rock pile, with a place for the smoke to go up through a hole that was surrounded by more stuck-together rocks. The Indian built his lodge fire in the center of his building allowing the smoke to drift around, up, and finally out through an opening in the rooftop.

A long table with benches were placed close to the fire pit. Soft coverings were spread on the floor over gleaming smooth boards. Through another door Tree Tall saw something big and black. Jerome's mother was stirring a pot that sat on the black thing. He remembered her using that same pot in the camp where they had lived for a time close by his village.

Steps were made against one wall leading to another floor above their heads. The white man had said the sleeping rooms were up there. Tree Tall thought that strange. His people slept and cooked all in the same room.

Holes in the walls were covered with what looked like clear ice. He could see through it. Cloth hung on each side making them pleasant to look through to the outside. The boy thought of Little Pine. How happy his mother would be to have such a lodge.

The woman came from the other room wiping her hands on a cloth. "Why, Tree Tall! How nice to see you again."

There was suddenly a noise above their heads. The Indian boy and girl backed toward the door as Jerome and his sister came thundering down the steps to greet them. "Tree Tall! How did you find us?" the white boy asked.

"You might say he ran into me—again," Jerome's father said with a laugh.

After eating with the white family Tree Tall and Jerome went outside. The Indian boy had watched everything Jerome did while eating at the long table. He had eaten with them before when they camped close by his village, but he still found using the fork and spoon difficult. Bright Sky had trouble too. That helped Tree Tall's pride a bit. The white people might find sharing a meal with his family just as strange. Jerome's sister took Bright Sky up the steps to the floor above when Jerome and Tree Tall went outside.

The two boys sat on the wooden steps by the door to talk. Before them was the long path of Oregon City with houses and stores on each side. Soon Jerome's father joined them. They listened to Tree Tall as he told in faltering English how the white trappers had captured him and of his escape after praying to Jesus. He then told about the soldiers who had ridden into their village to take them to the reservation. He told how their names had been changed and of wearing the old cast-off clothes of the whites.

"Soldiers think our skin same so all Indians friends." Tree Tall shook his head. "Not so! Tribes enemies long time. We not big tribe now. Many die from white man's sickness. Bigger tribes see Tree Tall and his people as nothing."

The man nodded. "That happens. Just because a person looks a little different, or is smaller, or new to a place, some feel they are of no account. God wants us to treat others the way we want them to treat us. We aren't to look down on people. We are to respect them as we respect ourselves."

"Respect?" Tree Tall tried the new word on his tongue questioningly.

"That means to think well of someone or yourself," the man explained. "God made you. He wants you to respect what he has made as good and to think well of yourself just the way you are. You are to think well of other people, too. You might not like some of the things they do, but you are not to feel they are no good just because they are different."

Tree Tall nodded. "Great Father Spirit very wise. But—" He stopped, remembering the things that had happened. "For time Tree Tall angry with Jesus and his Father, after white soldiers come. Think," he pointed to his head, "Father God not care about Tree Tall's people."

"He cares." The man gripped the boy's shoulder. "And so do we. He brought you to us didn't he? I've been trying to think of some way to help your family. Tomorrow, though, I believe I should take you back to your father and mother."

The boy seemed uncertain. "Like see mother, father, grandmother. But have fear." He glanced toward the door. "No want Bright Sky see fear. She brave, wise, she think."

Jerome smiled. "Just like a girl!"

"Now," said the man, "there you both go. Just because Bright Sky is different—a girl—you think she's not as good as you."

90

Jerome looked down. "I hadn't thought of it that way."

"Tree Tall," the man spoke again, "what did you do with the clothes the soldiers gave you to wear?"

The Indian boy smiled now. "In river. For fish. Too big legs. Too tight arms." He rubbed his legs and an arm.

"How would you like a pair of Jerome's pants and a shirt that's still good?"

Tree Tall looked down at his loin-piece. "Not like be tied in whiteskins'—in white man's—cloth."

"But the soldiers will make you wear their clothes again, won't they?" Jerome questioned.

The Indian boy nodded. He thought for a minute. "Be good wear friend Jerome's pants, shirt. But wait? Wait till come to reservation?"

"Yes," the man agreed. "We'll find a dress for Bright Sky, too. Something still good that Jerome's sister has outgrown."

Tree Tall looked up at the man. "Does Father God and Son hear with ears only white words? Tree Tall not know many white words to say when pray."

"God knows all languages," the man said. "He knows all things. You may pray in your people's words, if that's what you're asking."

The Indian boy smiled. "Good! Have many more things to pray now."

"God knows your thoughts, Tree Tall, as well as your words. He knows what's in your heart."

That night the white woman fixed a place for Tree Tall and Bright Sky to lie down in the sleeping rooms of Jerome and his sister. It seemed strange to sleep inside a building again. The last time Tree Tall had slept inside was the night before the soldiers had led them away from their village. The boy realized he should have stayed to help his father build a lodge on the reservation. He would do that when he got back with his family.

He thought about Jesus then. He did not feel anger anymore. "Thank you," Tree Tall whispered in the darkness, this time using his people's words, "for bringing Bright Sky and me to Jerome's family. I long to see my mother and father again. Even my grandmother will be welcome to my eyes. Forgive Tree Tall for anger. Thank you for hearing Indian words. Now I know you love my people, too. All people."

The next morning after an early meal, Jerome's mother packed some new-looking clothing for Tree Tall and Bright Sky. Then she and Jerome's sister went to open the store. Jerome's father loaded boxes in his wagon hitched behind two heavy black horses. Tree Tall touched the neck of one of the horses as he waited. How he would like to have such an animal!

Bright Sky did not seem to mind going to the reservation. But then, Tree Tall reasoned, she had never lived there before. Jerome climbed into the wagon with his father and the two Indian children. Bright Sky sat on the high seat beside the white man and the two boys made seats for themselves on boxes in the back. With a slap of the lines the man started the horses off at a trot, the iron-rimmed wheels rumbling the wagon out of town over the dry, hard-packed earth. Jerome explained to Tree Tall how his father had traded their oxen for the horses after reaching Oregon City. Tree Tall was glad.

They followed a dirt road that led back in the direction from where Tree Tall and Bright Sky had come. That night they made camp and Tree Tall helped Jerome picket the horses out to graze. On the fourth evening they rolled into the Indian encampment on the reservation. Tree Tall was back again—in the center of all he had come to dread. The boys who had pushed him around before he had run away watched now in silence as he jumped off the wagon.

Little Pine saw her son first. She ran to him, hugging and then scolding him for running away. His grandmother followed, adding words to those of his mother. Tree Tall knew it was only because they loved him. He was glad to be back with them.

Gray Seal came toward him more slowly,

hobbling on his forked pole. Tree Tall's heart sank. His father wore an old, ragged shirt and too-short pants of the whiteskins. "You have decided to return?" his father asked. "Did you think you were the only unhappy one here?"

Tree Tall shook his head. "It was just that I—"

"I know," Gray Seal spoke. He looked into his son's eyes with understanding. He glanced then at the white man who still sat on the high wagon seat.

"The whiteskins are Jerome and his father," Tree Tall explained. "They became my friends while we still lived in our village. The girl is one I found and helped after I left here."

Bright Sky, still wearing the buckskin garment of the enemy tribe from far across the mountains, scrambled over the seat to the back of the wagon with Jerome as though trying to hide from the stares of those who watched.

Gray Seal's eyes narrowed. "These whiteskins are the ones you would sneak away to see?"

Tree Tall swallowed hard. "I did not know you knew."

Jerome's father climbed down from the wagon. He took the boxes from the back, placing them on the ground in front of Gray Seal and Little Pine. "I thought you might be able to use these when you build your new lodge here."

Tree Tall's family did not understand. His grandmother backed away from the whiteskin.

94

Bright Sky and Jerome watched from the back of the wagon as Gray Seal cautiously looked at the contents of the boxes. With Tree Tall's help the white man explained how to use the hammer, nails, and axe. Gray Seal seemed interested. There was a sharp metal-bladed knife, too.

Gray Seal picked up the knife, turning it over in his hand. "These are new?" he asked. "Not whiteskin's throwaways?"

Tree Tall spoke Gray Seal's words and the white man nodded. "Some are new. Some are things I've had. The knife is from my store."

Hearing that, Gray Seal turned to Little Pine and spoke so the others could not hear. She ran to their lean-to returning with some of her best baskets and two new carved wooden bowls. Gray Seal took them, thrusting them into the white man's hands. "You bring some new things. Not all castaways of whiteskins. Gray Seal and Little Pine will pay for them with some new and some old things."

Taking the offered items, the white man nodded. He looked more closely then at the baskets and the bowls. "Who made these?" He looked at Tree Tall.

"Little Pine make baskets. One she give, her favorite. Use to cook berries. Gray Seal carve many things. Nothing in store so beautiful, Tree Tall think."

The white man looked more closely at the baskets and the
bowls. "Who made these?" he asked.

"You're right," the man said. "Could I see some other things your parents have made?"

Tree Tall told his father what the white man wanted. Gray Seal motioned for them all to follow him back to their lean-to. After looking over the baskets and the many carvings of Gray Seal, the white man smiled.

"Ask your parents if they would make things for me to sell in my store," he said to Tree Tall. "I will pay for what they make with food and new clothes your family can use. That way you will not need so many of the handouts of the white soldiers."

The boy spoke the white man's words to his father. Gray Seal leaned heavily on the forked pole as he listened. When Tree Tall finished, his father appeared to stand taller. He looked at Little Pine. She nodded and smiled.

Gray Seal straightened, holding his head higher as he turned to the white man. "We will do it!" he spoke.

Tree Tall relayed his father's words to Jerome's father, remembering the man saying how we all need to respect ourselves. Perhaps Gray Seal could start now to feel better about himself once again. Tree Tall smiled. Maybe things would be good again.

But then he thought about Bright Sky. What was going to happen to the girl? Who would take care of her now that he was with his family?

10

A New Way

TREE TALL turned to his father. "The girl."
He pointed toward the wagon where Bright Sky
and Jerome still waited. "I found her at a place
where a warlike tribe fought with the people she
was with. Her family is dead. Can she stay with
us?"

Gray Seal's eyes hardened. "No!"

Even Little Pine appeared set against the
idea. Tree Tall had thought his mother might
welcome a daughter into their family.

He looked at Jerome's father. "Bright Sky—"
The boy shook his head. "Not want here." Then
turning to his own father again, Tree Tall said,
"There is no one left to take care of her."

"That is no concern of ours," said Gray Seal.
"Let the whiteskin feed her. She can work as his
slave."

Jerome's father guessed what was being said. "We'll camp here with the soldiers tonight. I'll take Bright Sky back with me tomorrow. There's a mission school close by Oregon City. She'll be happier there with other Indian children who know her ways."

Tree Tall nodded. He did not know what a mission school was. He remembered the white trappers had asked if he had learned their words at a mission. Tree Tall wondered if the girl would indeed be happier there. Maybe, if Gray Seal learned the girl's family had been members of their tribe, he would change his mind. Bright Sky was, after all, still wearing the buckskin garment of the enemy.

"Could Bright Sky eat with us tonight before the white man takes her away tomorrow?" he asked Gray Seal.

His father hesitated, looking again at the girl in the wagon. At last he nodded.

Tree Tall went to get Bright Sky. Jerome handed him the bundle of clothing his mother had given the two Indian children. "The soldiers over there have been watching. Maybe you should put these on right away."

Tree Tall took the bundle and then Jerome and his father drove their wagon down to the soldier's camp. Tree Tall led the girl back to the lean-to where they took turns changing into the white man's clothes.

99

Bright Sky was quiet as Little Pine and Tree Tall's grandmother fixed their evening meal. The boy heard the older woman grumble to Little Pine, "I do not like having this strange girl here."

"Why do you not like me?" Bright Sky spoke up.

Gray Seal turned toward the girl. "You speak with our words. But you are of an enemy tribe."

"The tribe I was with was not mine," the girl said. "My father was as you and Tree Tall. When he and my mother died I was sold to work for another tribe. I was traded to them for a pinto pony."

Tree Tall's grandmother and mother had stopped their work. They both looked at the girl. The older woman asked, "What was the name of your father?"

"Running Deer," the girl replied.

Little Pine turned to Gray Seal. "Running Deer was a part of our tribe, but of another village. They lived close to us before we moved the last time—before you were hurt. I was told all his family died of the whiteskins' sickness."

Gray Seal nodded. "That must have been a lie so we would not know the girl had been traded away."

Bright Sky looked from one to the other. "You knew my father?"

"Yes," Little Pine said. "He was a friend. I

was close to your mother at one time. I was there when you were born."

Bright Sky asked many questions about her family as they ate. Later Tree Tall said he wanted to go visit the white boy Jerome for a while. He took Bright Sky with him. He wanted to give his parents time to talk. Maybe they would decide to keep the girl with them after all.

But as they started to leave, Gray Seal spoke to Bright Sky. "You come back. Stay the night here, before whiteskin takes you away in morning."

Tree Tall's heart sank. He was beginning to think of her as his sister. It looked as if that would never be now.

On the way to the white soldiers' camp he and the girl walked past the many cooking fires of the Indians. Tree Tall wondered at Bright Sky's quietness. "I am not used to your tongue being so still."

"You are not going to a mission school," the girl replied. "I have heard of it. They make you forget your people's ways. They teach you to live as the white man. But Bright Sky is Indian. Not white. Never will be white. Think if an Indian girl learns only the white man's ways, then she is nothing. She is still not white and maybe she is then no more Indian."

Just then several boys, some who had taunted

101

Tree Tall before he ran away from the reservation, stood barring the way. Speaking with the white words, since Tree Tall did not know the words of these boys, he told them, "No fight. All Indians. All brothers with the skin of red-brown. Not good Tree Tall stand against you. Not good you stand against Tree Tall."

The boys stopped, looking at him strangely. One stepped forward, pointing at his mouth. "White—words?" he questioned.

Tree Tall nodded. "Learned from friends. Will teach you, if want learn."

The boy who had questioned Tree Tall looked at the other boys, then nodded. "Soldiers say—go school. Talk—only white words." Silently the boys stood back, allowing Tree Tall and Bright Sky to pass.

"Tomorrow," said Tree Tall, as he and the girl started on again. "By river. Help you talk the white words. Tell of Oregon City, white man's village."

Later, after talking with Jerome for a while, Tree Tall and Bright Sky walked back to the lean-to. That night as Tree Tall lay on his fur robe he thought about Bright Sky's unhappiness. Then he remembered how Jesus had answered his prayers lately. "If you hear me now, Jesus," he whispered, "then please help Bright Sky. She is really not so bad for a girl."

The next morning after eating, Jerome and

his father walked over to the lean-to. "We're ready to start back," the white man said. "You must come now, Bright Sky."

Gray Seal stood up. He had been sitting by the small fire where Little Pine had cooked their morning meal. He stood without using the forked pole for the first time since he had been hurt.

"Tell the whiteskin," he said to Tree Tall, "that Bright Sky will stay with us. She will become the daughter of Little Pine. She will learn to make the baskets as you learn to do the work of the man. Tell the whiteskin we will live as proud people again—even here on reservation land."

Tree Tall's dark eyes sparkled with happiness as he related Gray Seal's words. Bright Sky gasped, then jumped up and down. Jerome and his father smiled.

Then, tucking his chin down close to his chest, the white man spoke aloud. "Thank you, Father, for helping Bright Sky and this family. Thank you in Jesus' name."

Jerome and his father then bid them goodbye. They said they would return soon with new clothes and other things to trade for the baskets and wooden carvings. Gray Seal looked at Tree Tall as they left.

"What did the whiteskin say with his head tucked down to his chest?"

The boy smiled. "He was thanking Jesus, the Son of the Great God who made everything, for helping us."

"Who is this Jesus?" Gray Seal asked.

"I will tell you about him," Tree Tall said, "as we work together building our new lodge. And as I learn to carve the wood with you."

He glanced at Bright Sky then. "Hello there, little sister."

The girl smiled. "Hello to you, brother-who-thinks-he-is-so-big." Bright Sky's black eyes danced as she teased him once again.

Tree Tall sighed. He supposed he would hear more from Bright Sky's smart tongue. But he really did not mind. He would be working with his father. They would become close for the first time since Gray Seal had been hurt. It would be good.

He could hardly wait to show Gray Seal a place he had seen back in the trees away from the main encampment. He had gone there several times to be alone before he ran away. It would be a good place to build a lodge. Maybe Spotted Elk would build his lodge there too.

Yes, the boy decided, life would be good once again.

Shirlee Evans lives in the Pacific Northwest, where her mother's family came as settlers in 1846. It was such settlers who squeezed the Indians off their land. But Shirlee also possesses an Indian heritage from her father who is one eighth Cherokee.

Today she and her husband live on land shared by the beavers and other wild creatures near Battle Ground, Washington, about 30 miles southwest of Mount St. Helens. It was here they raised their two sons. As a grandmother of six now, Shirlee enjoys helping her husband, Bob, with his draft horse hobby and driving their team.

While raising their sons she free-lanced for Christian and horseman magazines, besides having a teen novel, *Robin and the Lovable Bronc,* published by Moody Press. After her sons were grown she went to work for a weekly newspaper, refining her writing and winning a state Sigma Delta Chi award for investigative reporting. Her education consists of high school plus a few college classes, along with a great deal of life experience.

Before leaving the newspaper she interviewed Bill Towner, a Siletz Indian of Oregon, who with others of his disbanded tribe was seeking reinstatement by the United States government. (This has since come to realization.) Towner's story of the hardships suffered by his people over 100 years before at the hands of white soldiers and settlers etched itself on Shirlee's heart. Had her pioneer ancestors taken part in those acts?

Then, in 1983, a camp director from Royal Ridges Retreat, a Christian organization where two of her grandchildren were enrolled in day camp, asked Shirlee to write an Indian adventure story for their use. And so the fictional tale of Tree Tall, complete with historic highlights, came to be written.

Shirlee was born near Centralia, Washington. She manages to write several hours each day while working at Kris' Hallmark Shop near Vancouver, Washington. She is a member of Brush Prairie Conservative Baptist Church.